Bullying Me

by: CLAYBIGMAC

Gotham Books
30 N Gould St.
Ste. 20820, Sheridan, WY 82801
https://gothambooksinc.com/

Phone: 1 (307) 464-7800

© 2022 Claybigmac. All rights reserved.
No part of this book may be reproduced, stored in a retrieval system, or transmitted by any means without the written permission of the author.

Published by Gotham Books (November 10, 2022)

ISBN: 979-8-88775-136-8 (sc)
ISBN: 979-8-88775-137-5 (e)

Because of the dynamic nature of the Internet, any web addresses or links contained in this book may have changed since publication and may no longer be valid.

The views expressed in this work are solely those of the author and do not necessarily reflect the views of the publisher, and the publisher hereby disclaims any responsibility for them.

BULLIES

Please know we can still be friends.
It is never too late to say you are sorry.
One day you will need my helping hand and when you do,
you will reach up and know, that I am real.

"Happiness begins in the Heart!" ~ Claybigmac

I was running from you, feeling so blue while hurting in my heart. You were bullying me and teasing me making me fall apart.

Then in your ways to my amaze you fell from your bike.

Now watching you stuck in the glue this
I really like.
Yes, in quicksand you did land,
now you are not so smart.

Place your hand on your heart
and you will start to see that
I am real. Stuck in the sand not
how you had planned,
can you see this is a big deal?

By bullying me and teasing me you gave me lots of troubles. But now you must trust in me to set you free, as there are lots of bubbles. Please reach for my hand and understand how you made me feel?

Yes, I was so sad when you were so mad, it gave me such a fright.

When you joked around and pulled me down, holding my arm so tight.

Making me freeze as you did tease,
do you know bullying is not good?
Please do not cry, look in my eye and
I will help you like I should.
You must be quick, it`s not a trick
please reach up and make it right.

Now hold on tight, you must not fight
as you can plainly see.
That I am really your friend for in the end
caring is the key.

You are starting to slip, please grab a grip
and hold on tightly to my hand.
Then on the count of three,
let me see if I can free you from the sand?

Now you are aware that I really do care, can you please stop bullying me?

As I have helped you out without a doubt,
by giving you, my hand.
Yes, I used my strength at arm's length,
to free you from the sand.

Now best friends together. Yes, now and forever for everyone to see. That you played your part by giving your heart and the truth has set you free.

How you trusted in me to let it be.
Yes, you really do understand.

Yes, we are happy inside, playing with pride,
helping and caring like a good friend.
Life is much better this way,
feeling happy each day.
Good friendship we have shown.

Reflection Time

1. What does bullying mean to you?

Answer: _____

2. How did the person being bullied feel inside?

Answer: _____

3. Why is bullying not good?

Answer: _____

4. What should we do if we feel bullied?

Answer: _____

5. Do you think they are good friends now and why?

Answer: _____

"Happiness begins in the Heart!" ~ Claybigmac

www.ingramcontent.com/pod-product-compliance
Lightning Source LLC
LaVergne TN
LVHW070536070526
838199LV00075B/6792